THE NIGHT BEFORE
CHRISTMAS
IN
the South

Barbara G. S. Hagerty

ILLUSTRATED BY

SHERYL DICKERT

GIBBS SMITH
TO ENRICH AND INSPIRE HUMANKIND

'Twas a week before Christmas,
   that magical day
when wishes come true and children
   are at play.
Up North, toiling nonstop,
   the elves and the Clauses
worked 24/7, avoiding long pauses.

One day Santa grew quite
concerned for his wife.
All work and no play
makes for such a dull life.
He rose and embraced
his most dutiful bride.
"Let's hitch up the sleigh, Hon,
and go for a ride!"

"Santa, I feared that you
     might not remember:
we've not had a day off
     since early September!
Let's take a quick trip below
     the Mason-Dixon Line,
where the livin' is easy,
     the weather is fine!"

H is adorable spouse—
he knew her so well:
at heart Mrs. Claus was
a true Southern Belle.
"Off to the land of gray moss
and sweet tea—
it's a pre-Christmas frolic
for you and for me!"

"Let's both change our clothes—
    it would probably be wise
to make such a trip
    in civilian disguise.
Just one reindeer's needed—
    our load will be light.
Let's head to the South, then,
    on this very night!"

By early next dawn,
  Virginia came into view:
The Blue Ridge, the beaches,
  the Tidewater, too.
Cavaliers, plantations and
  history galore,
Mt. Vernon, Monticello,
  and a fun Christmas store.

They dropped down to Richmond,
   gave Rudolph a rest,
strolled Monument Ave.—
   Southern grandeur at its best!
"Eight presidents hailed from
   the great Old Dominion.
It's a wonderful place—
   that's my honest opinion."

"Virginia is so wondrous!
    Now, up and away,
There's much more to do
    on this vacation day.
Look below, dear—
    the scene couldn't be finer!"
They spied beautiful, emerald
    North Carolina.

The Outer Banks, Great Smokies,
  cities between:
Raleigh and Durham and Charlotte,
  "the Queen."
Kitty Hawk, Tweetsie Railroad,
  Carolina Blue.
Duke Blue Devils! Red clay!
  Pines trees! Barbecue!

"**I**'m hankering, Nick, for some
good Southern fare—
warm corn bread, fried chicken,
  hush puppies to share."
They alighted then, on
  South Carolina's Grand Strand,
munched on a feast, danced
  "the Shag" on the sand!

Back up in the sky, they spotted
  cities so fine:
Columbia and Greenville and
  Charleston—sublime!
They soared over Gamecocks,
  Tigers and more beaches,
With soul music, palmettos
  and fantastic peaches.

Then on down to Georgia—
   historic Savannah,
Then Athens and Macon and
   modern Atlanta.
From pecans to 'gators to
   skyscrapers tall,
from Bulldogs to Braves—
   this great state has it all!

"Oh, Santa," cried Mrs. Claus,
  "what would you think
of joining some revelers and
  having a drink?"
Gliding onto Peachtree in
  a masterful stroke,
said Santa, "It's Buckhead;
  we'll refresh with a Coke."

"That sure hit the spot!
  Now buckle up, dear.
North to proud Tennessee
  and still more good cheer.
It simply must be the most
  musical state:
The talent's amazing;
  the variety's great!"

"My darling," she asked,
"how do fans ever choose
among Elvis, Grand Ole Opry,
and Memphis's Blues?
There's Rock City, Ruby Falls,
Lookout Mountain, of course."
"Look! I see Dollywood and a
Tennessee walking horse!"

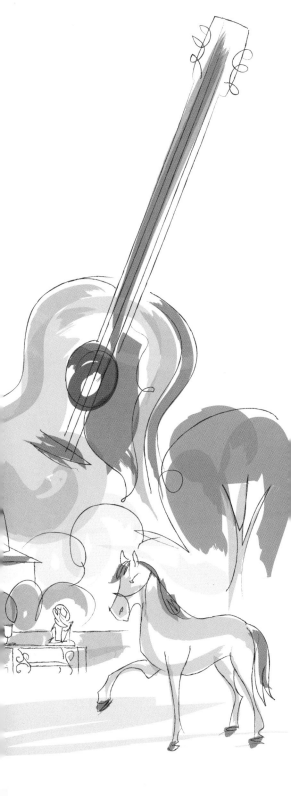

"To visit Tennessee," he said,
 "is our marvelous luck.
There's the Chattanooga Choo Choo
 and the Peabody ducks.
The Commodores and Volunteers
 are fabulous teams
in this agricultural state, so
 pleasant and green."

Santa glanced at his watch—
"Let's hurry to see
Sweet Home Alabama—
   in the 'Heart of Dixie!'"
They spied Auburn's Tigers and
   the Birmingham Zoo.
Montgomery and Huntsville and
   fair Mobile, too!

Great hunting and fishing
   are opportunities for fun,
plus Space Camp—it's geared to
   folks both old and young.
But what really opened the Clauses'
   eyes wide
was a glimpse of the bold,
   legendary Crimson Tide!

"What fun to watch football,
  to cheer 'Yippee Yippee.'
But we must make our way now
  over to Mississippi!"

Soon both the Clauses fell
headlong in love
with antebellum mansions,
    riverboats viewed from above.

Rebels! Magnolias! Hoop skirts!
    Catfish and more—
Mississippi had everything they'd
    ever wished for!
Vicksburg and Jackson, Biloxi
    and Tupelo,
and wide "Ol' Man River"
    a-coursing below!

Next up, Louisiana—
Let the good times roll!
They were envisioning next year
away from the Pole:
Zydeco, Cajuns, New Orleans,
and jazz,
Mardi Gras, costumes, parades,
razzmatazz!!

This time it was Santa who
  proposed something to eat.
"Pralines and Po' Boys
  would be quite a treat."
Descending, they joined a happy
  holiday crowd
that was shouting "Geaux, Tigers"
  incredibly loud!

They were having a good time
     indulging themselves,
when suddenly Santa remembered
     the elves.
"We can't fail the children—
     quick, we must go
back home to our workshop
     Up North in the snow."

Their time in the South had been
such a fine gift.
Hospitality and charm gave them
both a big lift.
In fondness, Santa snuggled and
hugged his best girl.
He told Rudolph to twirl
to the top of the world.

Santa knew the best present:
spend time with each other,
give of ourselves and love
one another!
As Santa and Mrs. C. soared
out of sight,
He drawled, "Merry Christmas,
blessings, y'all have a good night!"

First Edition

18 17 16   5 4 3 2

Published by
Gibbs Smith
P.O. Box 667
Layton, Utah 84041

1.800.835.4993 orders
www.gibbs-smith.com

Designed and illustrated by Sheryl Dickert

Special thanks to Nathalie Dupree
for inspiration and support

Printed and bound in China
Gibbs Smith books are printed on either
recycled, 100% post-consumer waste, FSC-
certified papers or on paper produced from
sustainable PEFC-certified forest/controlled
wood source. Learn more at www.pefc.org.

Library of Congress Cataloging-in-Publication Data

Hagerty, Barbara G.S.
  The night before Christmas in the South /
Barbara G.S. Hagerty ; illustrated by
Sheryl Dickert. — First edition.
      pages cm
  ISBN 978-1-4236-3638-0
1. Christmas poetry. 2. Southern
States—Poetry. I. Dickert, Sheryl,
illustrator. II. Title.
  PS3608.A375N66 2014
    813'.6—dc23
                              2014000646